Dear Parent:
Your child's love of reading starts here!

Every child learns to read in a different way and at his or her own speed. Some go back and forth between reading levels and read favorite books again and again. Others read through each level in order. You can help your young reader improve and become more confident by encouraging his or her own interests and abilities. From books your child reads with you to the first books he or she reads alone, there are I Can Read Books for every stage of reading:

SHARED READING
Basic language, word repetition, and whimsical illustrations, ideal for sharing with your emergent reader

BEGINNING READING
Short sentences, familiar words, and simple concepts for children eager to read on their own

READING WITH HELP
Engaging stories, longer sentences, and language play for developing readers

READING ALONE
Complex plots, challenging vocabulary, and high-interest topics for the independent reader

ADVANCED READING
Short paragraphs, chapters, and exciting themes for the perfect bridge to chapter books

I Can Read Books have introduced children to the joy of reading since 1957. Featuring award-winning authors and illustrators and a fabulous cast of beloved characters, I Can Read Books set the standard for beginning readers.

A lifetime of discovery begins with the magical words **"I Can Read!"**

Visit www.icanread.com for information
on enriching your child's reading experience.

I Can Read!

BEGINNING
1
READING

Fancy NANCY

Potpourri of Books

POISON IVY EXPERT

THE SHOW MUST GO ON

SPECTACULAR SPECTACLES

by Jane O'Connor

cover illustrations by Robin Preiss Glasser

interior illustrations by Ted Enik

HARPER

An Imprint of HarperCollinsPublishers

TABLE OF CONTENTS

I Can Read!

BEGINNING
1
READING

Fancy NANCY

Poison Ivy Expert

HARPER
An Imprint of HarperCollinsPublishers

Look!

I am picking

a bouquet of wildflowers.

(Bouquet is fancy

for a bunch of flowers.)

"Watch out for poison ivy,"

Mom keeps warning me.

"I am! I am!" I say.

I know what poison ivy looks like.

I know the rhyme.

"Leaves of three. Let it be."

Why, I am practically

a poison ivy expert.

The next day

I bring the bouquet to school.

Bree brings cupcakes.

Robert brings purple punch.

We conceal everything.

(Conceal is a fancy word for hide.)

We are having a surprise party

for Ms. Glass.

It is her birthday!

By lunchtime

I am so excited about the surprise

that I get all itchy.

My arms itch.

My nose itches.

Every inch of me itches!

"Nancy, you have red bumps

on your face," Bree says.

I do?

Yes! I do!

Ms. Glass calls home.

Dad picks me up

and we go to the doctor.

Can you guess what is wrong?

Yes! I have poison ivy.

It is all my fault!

I am not a poison ivy expert
after all.

And what if my bouquet
had poison ivy in it?

Dad lets me call Ms. Glass.

"There is no poison ivy,"

she tells me.

"Just beautiful flowers.

Merci, Nancy."

(Ms. Glass knows I love French.)

She hopes I am better soon.

Later, Bree stops by.

I am too itchy for company.

So she sends stuff over

in our mail basket.

A note from Ms. Glass says,

"Everyone is starting a journal.

You can write yours at home."

Bree's note says,

"Thursday is Picture Day.

Will you be back?"

No, I won't be back Thursday!

I am miserable.

(That's even worse than unhappy,
and also much fancier.)

All night I itch and itch.

The next morning

I am exhausted.

That is fancy for very, very tired.

Mom shows me a little jar.

It is from the lady next door.

"Mrs. DeVine says to put

this cream on your bumps,"

Mom tells me.

"It is a home remedy."

A remedy is fancy for medicine.

Ooh la la! I don't itch.

What is this magic cream?

Mrs. DeVine says

it has jewelweed in it.

Jewelweed grows in her garden.

I like the name!

Weeds are not fancy.

But jewelweed sure sounds fancy!

Mom brings home a library book.

I learn about poison ivy.

Then I start my journal.

I put in many fascinating facts.

(Fascinating is fancy

for interesting.)

In the fall, poison ivy turns red.

It looks very beautiful.

But don't let that fool you.

Stay away!

summer

fall

Dogs are lucky.
If they touch poison ivy,
nothing happens to them.

My dog, Frenchy

If you touch a person
with poison ivy,
you will NOT catch it.
Just don't touch clothes
that still have poison ivy on them.

By Sunday

I really am a poison ivy expert.

Tomorrow I go back to school.

Yippee!

In the afternoon
I go to Bree's house.

Ooh la la!

There is a surprise party,

for me!

There are cookies and punch.

And we all dance

to an old rock and roll song.

Guess what it's called?

"Poison Ivy."

Fancy Nancy's Fancy Words

These are the fancy words in this book:

Bouquet—a bunch of flowers

Conceal—hide

Exhausted—very, very tired

Fascinating—interesting

Merci—"thank you" in French (you say it like this: mair-SEE)

Miserable—very unhappy

Remedy—medicine

Fancy NANCY

The Show Must Go On

HARPER

An Imprint of HarperCollinsPublishers

"Quiet, please," says Ms. Glass.

"I have an announcement."

(That means she has something

important to tell us.)

"The talent show is in a week."

Yay! Bree and I bump fists.

We have our act planned out already.

We will wear fancy circus costumes.

We will sing a song.

It is about daring girls on a trapeze.

Then Ms. Glass says,

"I am assigning partners."

Oh no!

That means we don't get to choose!

I am not assigned to Bree.

I am assigned to Lionel.

He is very shy.

I hardly know him.

Ms. Glass wants us

to brainstorm with our partner.

That means to talk over ideas.

So I ask Lionel,

"Do you like to sing?"

He says no.

He does not like to dance

or tell jokes.

He can wiggle his ears.

He can crack his fingers.

He can balance a spoon on his nose.

"Very cool," I say.

"But I can't do those things.

We need to perform together."

(Perform is a fancy word for act.)

That night I say,

"Bree and Yoko are partners.

They will do a fan dance

and wear kimonos."

(I explain that a kimono

is a fancy Japanese robe.)

"Lionel and I
can't think of anything to do."
I sigh a deep sigh.
"And now I won't get to wear
my circus costume."

Mom says, "Ask Lionel over.

Get to know each other.

It will help you plan an act."

On Saturday I ask Lionel over.

But his mom can't drop him off.

So Dad drives me to Lionel's house.

Ooh la la! It is very fancy.

It is almost a mansion.

Lionel's room is huge.

(Huge is much bigger than big.)

There are lots of toy lions.

"Oh! I get it!" I say.

"You like lions

because your name is Lionel."

I pick up a little glass lion.

"This is adorable," I say.

I tell him I like fancy words.

And adorable is fancy for cute.

Lionel shows me a lion mask.

"Wow," I say. "It's great!"

He puts on the mask.

"Grrr," Lionel says, and chases me.

We race all over his house.

"Help! Help!" I yell.

Later we have snacks.

"You're a great lion," I tell Lionel.

Then I get an extremely great idea!

"Let's do a circus act.

You can be the lion.

I can be the lion tamer.

I already have a costume."

Lionel likes the idea. Yay!

The next week we get together

many times to rehearse.

(That's a fancy word for practice.)

Still, we are nervous
on the day of the show.
We hear Ms. Glass announce,
"Here is Lady Lulubell
and the man-eating lion!"

The curtain opens.

Lionel jumps through the hoop.

Lionel walks on a pretend tightrope.

Then he roars and chases me.

"Don't eat me!" I cry.

"Eat this instead!"

I hand Lionel a huge lollipop.

He starts licking it and purring.

Then I curtsy and he bows.

Our act is over.

There is a lot of applause!

(That's a fancy word for clapping.)

I hear my dad shout, "Bravo!"

We all go out for ice cream.

I give Lionel a clay lion I made.

And guess what?

He teaches me

to balance a spoon on my nose!

Fancy Nancy's Fancy Words

These are the fancy words in this book:

Adorable—cute

Announcement—something important to tell

Applause—clapping

Assign—to choose something for someone else

Brainstorm—to talk over lots of ideas

Bravo—way to go!

Kimono—fancy Japanese robe

Mansion—a very fancy house

Perform—to act (or dance or sing)

Rehearse—to practice

Fancy NANCY Spectacular Spectacles

HARPER

An Imprint of HarperCollinsPublishers

For Rob, who finally
got spectacles
—J.O'C.

For my sister Erica,
who sees us all
with such clarity
—R.P.G.

Re: Spectacles, the
otherwise wise Ms. Parker
was incorrectable.
—T.E.

Bree can't come over
after school today.
She is going to an eye doctor.

In school, her eyes hurt a lot.

It is very distressing.

(That's like upsetting—only fancier.)

I hope the eye doctor helps her.

That night,

Bree sends a note in our basket.

"I have a surprise," the note says.

I send back a note.

"Tell me! Tell me!" it says.

Bree sends another note.

"You have to wait until tomorrow."

I am not very good at waiting.

The next morning,

I race over to Bree's house.

Out she comes.

Bree is wearing glasses!

They are for reading.

Her eyes won't hurt anymore.

"Ooh la la!" I say.

"You look spectacular."

(That's a fancy word for great.)

Bree's glasses are lavender.

That's fancy for light purple.

And they glitter.

Bree puts her glasses
in a silver case.
Her glasses and case
are both so fancy!

At school,

Bree tells our class

about the eye doctor.

Bree had to read a chart

with lots of letters on it.

The letters went from big to tiny.

"Glasses are like magic.

I can read tiny stuff now," she says.

"Nothing looks blurry!"

"Your glasses are most becoming,"

Ms. Glass says.

That's a fancy word

I have never heard before.

Ms. Glass says it means pretty.

"I think Bree looks spectacular!"
I say.

Then Ms. Glass tells us

that spectacles is another word

for eyeglasses.

Wow! Bree has spectacular spectacles.

During math time,

Bree wears her glasses.

In the library,

she wears her glasses.

The eye doctor also gave Bree

a little silk hankie

for cleaning her glasses.

It is pink with purple polka dots.

I wish I had a hankie like that.

I wish I had a silver case.

Most of all,

I wish I had lavender glasses

with glitter.

Then I start to wonder.

Maybe I do need glasses.

At dinner,

I am pretty sure

my food looks blurry.

After dinner, I do a puzzle.

It has tiny pieces

and is very challenging.

(That's fancy for hard.)

I try squinting. Yes!

I do think everything

looks clearer now.

Later my mom comes into my room.

I am reading in the dark.

"That is very bad for your eyes!"

Mom says.

"I know," I say.

Then I tell Mom about Bree.

"I bet she'll get a fancy necklace,

like the one Ms. Glass wears.

It's not fair!" I say.

"I want glasses."

My mom does not get mad.

She says Bree has glasses because
her eyes need them.

"Your eyes are fine.

You are a lucky girl."

I know that, but I still want them.

Then I get an idea

that is spectacular.

My mom helps me.

My old sunglasses had only one lens.

So I popped out the other.

My glasses are just pretend.

But don't I look fancy?

Fancy Nancy's Fancy Words

These are the fancy words in this book:

Becoming—pretty

Challenging—hard

Distressing—very upsetting

Lavender—light purple

Spectacles—eyeglasses

Spectacular—great